chickaDEE

Eat it Up!

Lip-smacking recipes for kids

Recipes by Elisabeth de Mariaffi

Illustrations by Jay Stephens, Gabriel Morrissette and Brooke Kerrigan

Owl

Contents

Jack
The bully

A.J.

Nicole

Chick
Dee's best friend

Arf
The neighbourhood dog

Shelldon
Dee's little brother

THIS **SIGN** MEANS THE RECIPE WILL TAKE SOME TIME TO MAKE. DO IT ON A RAINY DAY OR DURING A PLAYDATE WITH A FRIEND!

Robin
Chick's big sister

Michael

Myris

Bruno
The friendly monster

Fang
The other bully

Dee
Chick's best friend

Petal
The monkey pal

Let's Stay Safe

Cooking is tons of fun, but it can be dangerous. Read these important tips:

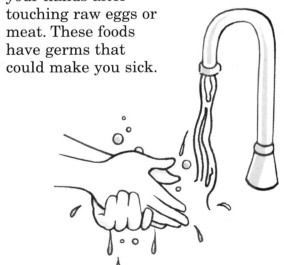

Ask an adult for permission and help

Not only is it fun to cook together, it takes less time.

Wash your hands

Your hands must be clean before you begin so germs don't get into the food. Always wash your hands after touching raw eggs or meat. These foods have germs that could make you sick.

Using sharp tools

- Ask an adult to cut hard food, like raw carrots.
- Always use one hand to hold the food you are cutting, and the other to hold the knife.

- Grate food slowly and carefully. Stop when your hand gets close to the grater.

- Never put your hand into a blender or food processor, even if it is turned off. Tip the bowl to get chopped food out.

in the Kitchen!

Using the stove or oven

- Wear fitted clothes and tie back long hair. Loose clothes may accidentally touch a hot element or gas flame and catch fire.

- Wear an apron to protect yourself from hot, splattering food. Heat oil or butter over medium heat so it doesn't splatter.

- An adult should be there to help you slide in or remove food from the oven. Always wear oven mitts.

- When you open a hot oven, stand back a bit to let the heat come out first.

- Turn the handle of your pan towards the back of the stove so it doesn't get knocked off by accident.

- Never touch a stove element because it stays hot for awhile after it's turned off.

Let's Get Equipped

Frying pans (small and large)

Apron

Bundt pan

Cookie sheet

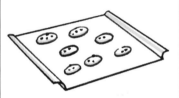

Ice pop moulds

Blender or food processor

Candy thermometer

Cutting board

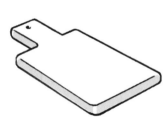

Knives – sharp ones for cutting, dinner knives for spreading

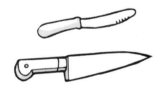

Box grater

Cookie cutters

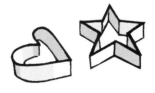

Electric mixer

Ladle

Loaf pan

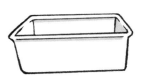

Oven mitts

Ramekins

Spatula

Measuring cups

Parchment paper

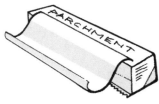

Rolling pin

Vegetable peeler

Measuring spoons

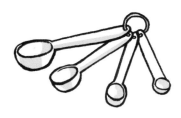

Pasta pot

Saucepans (small and large)

Whisk

Mixing bowls (small, medium and large)

Pitcher

Serving bowl

Wooden mixing spoon

Muffin pan

Pizza cutter

Sieve

Zester or small grater

Let's Get Cooking

Bake foods in a hot oven

Batter is a mixture that becomes solid when cooked

Beat an egg with a fork or whisk

Bite-sized pieces should fit easily in your mouth

Blend mixtures together like smoothies in a blender or food processor

Boil means to heat a liquid on high heat until it bubbles or to cook something in very hot water, like pasta

Chop or **cut** with a knife to make small pieces of food

Cook means using heat to prepare food

Cool baked goods on a cooling rack until they are room temperature

Drain means to remove cooking liquid from around food, such as water from cooked pasta

Fry foods in hot oil on a stove

Grate cheese or other foods into tiny pieces with a grater or zester

Grease a muffin pan or cookie sheet by rubbing it with butter or margarine

Heat foods up using a stove, oven or microwave

Ingredients are the foods and spices used in a recipe

Knead dough by pressing, pushing and pulling it with your hands

Lumpy batter is not perfectly smooth

Measure foods with measuring cups or spoons to find the right amount

Melt food like butter, cheese or chocolate by heating until it turns into a liquid

Mix means to stir together

Pour something from one container into another

Preheat means to heat the oven ahead of time

Purée means to blend soft foods in a blender or food processor until smooth

Sauté foods quickly over high heat with a small amount of oil

Cooking Measurements

Metric		Imperial	
C	Celsius	F	Fahrenheit
cm	centimetre	in	inch
g	gram	lb	pound
mL	millilitre	oz	ounce
L	litre	tsp	teaspoon
		tbsp	tablespoon

Scrape all the batter out of a bowl with a rubber spatula so nothing is wasted

Serve your cooked food to the hungry people who want to eat it

Simmer means to keep heated food just below the boiling point

Stir ingredients together by mixing with a spoon or fork

Thaw means to let frozen food warm up to room temperature

Toss salad ingredients together in a bowl with salad servers

Whisk liquids together to mix them completely using a whisk or fork

Clean-up Tips

Cleaning up is part of cooking. If you leave a clean kitchen, your parents will want you to cook more often!

- Rinse bowls, plates, mixing spoons and other equipment as soon as you're done so the ingredients don't get hard and become difficult to clean.

- Fill a sink with warm, soapy water so you can soak your dirty dishes while you finish cooking.

- Wipe up counters with a damp cloth while you are cooking.

- Put ingredients away as soon as you are done with them.

- Sometimes you can strike a deal with a parent or sibling: they just may agree to wash the dishes if you do the cooking!

Wake

It's Breakfast

Up!
Time

Buttermilk Power Pancakes

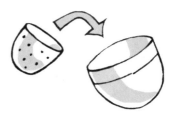

Makes: 12 to 16 pancakes

Prep: 25 minutes

You'll need:

Dry ingredients:

250 mL (1 cup) whole wheat flour

250 mL (1 cup) all-purpose flour

125 mL (½ cup) wheat germ

5 mL (1 tsp) baking soda

15 mL (1 tbsp) brown sugar

5 mL (1 tsp) salt

Wet ingredients:

2 large eggs

500 to 625 mL (2 to 2½ cups) buttermilk

30 mL (2 tbsp) butter, melted

1. **Stir** all dry ingredients together in large mixing bowl.

2. In small bowl, **beat** eggs. Stir in buttermilk.

3. Add wet ingredients to dry ingredients and stir. **Stir** in butter. Don't worry if mixture is lumpy.

ARF TURNED **BLUE** BECAUSE SHE EATS SO **MUCH** OF THIS **SAUCE!**

Yummy Blueberry Sauce

Makes: about 2 cups	
Prep: 10 minutes	

You'll need:

300 g (10 oz) frozen blueberries, thawed
125 mL (½ cup) maple syrup
15 mL (1 tbsp) lemon juice
15 mL (1 tbsp) cornstarch

1. Combine all ingredients in medium saucepan.

2. Bring to a **boil** over medium heat, stirring occasionally. Lower heat and let **simmer** for 2 minutes.

3. Remove from heat. **Serve** warm.

4. **Heat** pan to medium-high. Ladle 2 or 3 pancakes into pan.

5. When edges look dry and bubbles appear on top, flip pancakes over and cook for another minute or so. Repeat until batter is gone.

spizzle

6. **Serve** with maple syrup or Yummy Blueberry Sauce.

Bruno's
Breakfast Bake

Makes: 4 servings

Prep: 25 minutes

You'll need:

50 mL (¼ cup) chopped ham, plus extra for garnish

4 large or extra-large eggs

pinch of salt and pepper

20 mL (4 tsp) cream

50 mL (¼ cup) grated cheddar cheese

GRRR!

DON'T WORRY!

THAT'S JUST MY *TUMMY!* I'M A FRIENDLY MONSTER!

1. **Preheat** oven to 180°C (350°F). Grease 4 ramekins.

2. Spoon 15 mL (1 tbsp) of ham into bottom of each ramekin.

3. Crack 1 egg and beat in bowl. Add salt and pepper. Pour egg into ramekin. Repeat for remaining ramekins.

4. Top each with 5 mL (1 tsp) of cream and 15 mL (1 tbsp) of cheese.

5. Place ramekins on cookie sheet. **Bake** for 10 minutes or until egg sets.

6. Remove cookie sheet with oven mitts. Keep mitts on to place them on plates. Decorate with ham.

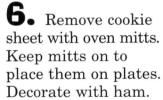

Shelldon's Eggeritos

Makes: 6 servings

Prep: 15 minutes

You'll need:

8 large eggs

45 mL (3 tbsp) milk

pinch of salt and pepper

10 mL (2 tsp) butter

84 g (3 oz) medium cheddar cheese, cubed

3 large whole wheat tortillas

CHUCK!

HI-YO EGGERITO!

1. Crack eggs into medium bowl. Add milk and **whisk** together. Add salt and pepper.

crack!

2. **Melt** butter in pan at medium-low until foamy. Add eggs. When they start to cook, add cheese and stir until done. Remove from heat.

3. Cut each tortilla in half. Place a scoop of eggs on each half, leaving space around the edges. Fold bottom up, then fold one side over the other. Secure with toothpick.

chickaDEE tip: Want to give your Eggerito some bite? Spice it up with a spoonful of salsa before you fold up your wrap!

Sweet Strawberries and Oranges in
Heavenly
Honey Cream

Makes: 4 servings

Prep: 10 minutes

You'll need:

45 mL (3 tbsp) cream

15 mL (1 tbsp) liquid honey

500 mL (1 pint) strawberries, washed, hulled and cut into bite-sized pieces

1 large seedless navel orange, peeled and cut into bite-sized pieces

1. Whisk cream and honey together in small bowl until completely blended.

2. Mix strawberries and oranges together in large bowl. Pour honey cream over fruit and stir. Serve immediately or refrigerate. Stir again before serving.

Smilin' Smoothies

SLURP!

SLOOP!

Makes: 2 smoothies

Prep: 5 minutes

You'll need:

For smoothie base:

250 mL (1 cup) plain yogurt

125 mL (1/2 cup) orange juice

15 mL (1 tbsp) honey

For mango smoothie, add:

250 mL (1 cup) ripe mango chunks, frozen

For strawberry-banana smoothie, add:

250 mL (1 cup) ripe banana chunks, frozen

125 mL (1/2 cup) strawberries, frozen

1. Put ingredients in blender or food processor and **blend** until smooth. If it's too thick, add some milk and blend again.

chickaDEE tip: Keep fruit in the freezer so you'll always be ready to make a Smilin' Smoothie! If you don't have frozen fruit, blend fresh fruit chunks with three or four ice cubes. It might be noisy, so plug your ears!

Robin's Marv-ilicious Muffins

Makes: 12 large muffins

Prep: 45 minutes

You'll need:

Dry ingredients:

375 mL (1½ cups) all-purpose flour

250 mL (1 cup) whole wheat flour

175 mL (¾ cup) packed brown sugar

15 mL (1 tbsp) baking powder

2 mL (½ tsp) salt

Wet ingredients:

2 large eggs

250 mL (1 cup) milk

125 mL (½ cup) unsalted butter, melted

MAKE MY MARV-ILICIOUS MUFFINS *THREE* DIFFERENT WAYS!

1. **Preheat** oven to 200°C (400°F). Line 12 muffin cups with paper liners.

2. **Mix** dry ingredients in large bowl and set aside. In small bowl, beat eggs lightly. **Stir** in milk and butter.

3. **Pour** wet ingredients into dry ingredients and stir well. Muffin batter likes to be **lumpy**.

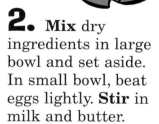
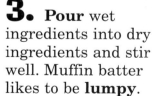

You Choose!

Blueberry

7 mL (1½ tsp) grated lemon rind

375 mL (1½ cups) fresh blueberries, *or* 300 g (10 oz) frozen blueberries, thawed

Pumpkin-Raisin

250 mL (1 cup) canned pumpkin purée

5 mL (1 tsp) cinnamon

2 mL (½ tsp) ginger

1 mL (¼ tsp) nutmeg

125 mL (½ cup) raisins

Banana-Chocolate Chip

3 ripe bananas, mashed

125 mL (½ cup) chocolate chips

Pick your favourite muffin, stir the ingredients together and then add them to your batter. See step 4 on this page.

4. Look at the *You Choose!* list and decide which muffins to make. **Stir** those ingredients into batter.

5. Spoon batter into each muffin cup. **Bake** for 20 minutes.

6. To check if your muffins are ready, insert a toothpick and make sure it comes out clean. If not, bake for 3 more minutes.

7. When muffins are done, place pan on cooling rack. After 10 minutes, slide muffins out of the pan and continue to cool.

chickaDEE tip: To measure 125 mL (½ cup) of butter, fill a clear, 500 mL (2 cup) measuring cup with 375 mL (1½ cups) of water. Now add small chunks of butter until the water reaches the 500 mL (2 cup) level. The amount of butter you have added equals exactly 125 mL (½ cup). Neat, huh?

Lip-Sm Sandwiches

acking
& Snacks

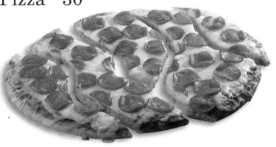

FIZZLE! FLIP! SCOOP! POP!

WHO WANTS THE FIRST "ROBIN SPECIAL"?

BLAH! YIPES!!

HUH?

TELL YOU WHAT, SIS. JUST LET US MAKE THE SANDWICHES TODAY!

END

Fang's Stuff 'Em Up Sandwiches

DON'T MAKE MY SANDWICHES! THEY'RE ALL FOR ME!

Makes:
8 snacks or 4 meals

Prep: 15 minutes

You'll need:

2 eggs

50 mL (¼ cup) milk

1 loaf egg bread, unsliced

butter or margarine

Filling choices:

nut butter, honey, banana slices and jam

ham and cheese

tomato, cheddar and pre-cooked bacon

1. Crack eggs into wide, shallow bowl and **beat** gently. Add milk and **stir**. Set aside.

2. Ask an adult to cut 4 slices of egg bread, about 5 cm (2 in) thick. Cut each slice into 2 triangles. Then, in each triangle, cut a horizontal slit almost to the crust.

3. Stuff triangles with your favourite fillings.

4. **Heat** large frying pan on medium-low. Add 10 mL (2 tsp) of butter. Dip each sandwich in egg mixture to coat both sides.

5. Add a few sandwiches to pan and press with spatula. **Cook** for 3 minutes per side until golden brown. Remove from pan.

6. Add 10 mL (2 tsp) of butter to pan and **cook** remaining sandwiches. Let them **cool** because the filling will be piping hot!

Cookie Cutter Grilled Cheese

Makes: 4 sandwiches

Prep: 10 minutes

You'll need:

butter

8 slices egg bread or another soft bread

8 sandwich-size slices cheddar cheese (or enough small slices to cover the bread)

SNIFF!
SNIFF!

AAAH!

1. Spread lots of butter on 1 side of each slice of bread.

2. Place 1 slice of bread, buttered side down, on cutting board. Arrange 2 or more slices of cheese on top of bread. Place another slice of bread, buttered side up, on top of cheese.

3. **Heat** frying pan on medium-low. When hot, place 2 sandwiches in pan. Press with spatula and cook for 2 to 3 minutes per side until cheese melts and bread is golden brown.

Stzzzz

4. Remove from pan and **cool** 3 minutes. Cook all sandwiches the same way.

5. Use cookie cutters to cut sandwiches into shapes. Make big shapes or use small cookie cutters to make **bite-sized** sandwiches!

Jack's Roll-Around Tuna Grab

I'M JUST BATTY FOR THESE!

Makes: 4 sandwiches

Prep: 15 minutes

You'll need:

2 cans water-packed tuna

50 mL (¼ cup) mayonnaise

30 mL (2 tbsp) minced celery

2 large tortillas

Optional:

15 mL (1 tbsp) relish

15 mL (1 tbsp) minced red onion

30 mL (2 tbsp) grated cheese

15 mL (1 tbsp) salsa

1. **Drain** and rinse tuna. Put in mixing bowl. Add celery, mayonnaise and any optional ingredients. Mash together with fork.

2. Soften tortillas in microwave for 10 seconds. Divide filling in half and place in middle of each tortilla. Fold ends over filling. Roll tightly, cut in half and serve.

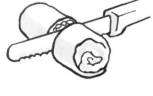

Skyscraper Sandwich

Makes: 1 large sandwich – enough for 2 kids or 1 hungry person!

Prep: 10 minutes

You'll need:

3 slices whole wheat or multi-grain bread

butter, optional

mustard, optional

sliced cold cuts such as Italian salami, prosciutto ham

sliced cheese such as provolone, or your favourite

sliced pickles

mayonnaise

sliced turkey breast

sliced tomatoes and lettuce

I COULD EAT *THREE* OF THESE!

1. On a slice of bread, spread butter or mustard. Layer cold cuts, cheese and pickle slices on this slice.

2. Spread a second slice of bread with mayonnaise and place on first slice. Now top second slice of bread with turkey. Add tomato and lettuce.

3. Add last slice of bread to make three layers. Cut sandwich into 2 triangles and spear each triangle with a fancy toothpick.

chickaDEE tip:
Make a Skyscraper Melt! Follow the steps above, but toast the bread and replace the lettuce with more tomato. Wrap the sandwich in tin foil and put in the oven at 180°C (350°F) for five minutes.

Build a Wacky Sandwich

Try these ingredients:

tuna salad
sliced hard-boiled eggs
mayonnaise
ketchup
sliced cheese
pastrami
turkey
cream cheese
avocado
potato chips
French fries
raisins
peanut butter
hot salsa
chicken fingers
chocolate syrup
jam
tiny pickles
grated carrots
lettuce
banana slices
bacon
salami
fish sticks

What crazy ingredients would you add to your wacky sandwich?

Lip-Smacking Sandwiches & Snacks   27

Chick and Dee's Handful of
Scrumptious
Snacks

Car Trip Crunch

Makes:	about 1.5 L (6 cups)
Prep:	1 hour

You'll need:

250 mL (1 cup) salted, mixed nuts

375 mL (1½ cups) small pretzels

1 L (4 cups) mixed, dry cereal (try a mix of your favourites)

50 mL (¼ cup) butter

1 mL (¼ tsp) garlic salt

1 mL (¼ tsp) onion salt

10 mL (2 tsp) Worcestershire sauce

5 mL (1 tsp) lemon juice

1. **Preheat** oven to 120°C (250°F). Line a rimmed cookie sheet with parchment paper. **Stir** nuts, pretzels and cereals in the pan.

2. **Melt** butter in saucepan and stir in rest of ingredients. Drizzle over cereal and nuts, and stir to coat evenly.

3. **Bake** for 45 minutes, stirring every 15 minutes. Store in sealed container for up to 2 months.

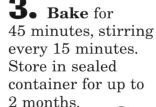

chickaDEE tip: To make a nut-free Car Trip Crunch, replace nuts with 250 mL (1 cup) of other ingredients such as salted soy nuts or mini-crackers.

ARF! ARF!

Pop 'Em! Pizza Popcorn

Makes: about 2 L (8 cups)

Prep: 10 minutes

You'll need:

50 mL (¼ cup) grated Parmesan cheese

5 mL (1 tsp) garlic powder

5 mL (1 tsp) Italian herb seasoning

5 mL (1 tsp) paprika

2 mL (½ tsp) salt, if using air-popped popcorn. If using microwave popcorn, do not add salt

pepper to taste

2 L (8 cups) fresh popcorn (either air-popped or *plain* microwave popcorn)

30 to 45 mL (2 to 3 tbsp) butter, melted

1. **Stir** Parmesan cheese, garlic powder, Italian seasoning, paprika, salt and pepper together in bowl.

2. **Toss** popcorn with melted butter. Add seasoning and mix thoroughly until popcorn is evenly coated.

Bird Seed

Mix together one of these combos:

salted, roasted sunflower seeds and raisins

roasted peanuts and raisins (also known as GORP, for Good Old Raisins and Peanuts)

roasted peanuts or cashews, dried apricots and roasted pumpkin seeds

dried apples, roasted pumpkin seeds, roasted cashews and raisins

Lickety-Split Pizza

OOF!

MAYBE I PUT ON **TOO** MUCH CHEESE!

Makes: 5 to 6 pizza strips

Prep: 15 minutes

You'll need:

1 jar pizza or tomato sauce

1 large pre-baked pizza crust

400 g (14 oz) grated mozzarella cheese

Choose toppings from this list or create your own:

Meats: pepperoni, sausage, ham, tuna, anchovies

Veggies: tomatoes, mushrooms, sweet or hot peppers, onions, broccoli

Fruit: sliced apples, pineapple

sliced hard-boiled eggs

sliced olives

crushed garlic

extra cheese

1. **Preheat** oven to 200°C (400°F).

2. Spread sauce on pizza crust, then add cheese and your favourite toppings. Place pizza on cookie sheet.

3. **Bake** for 5 minutes, then broil for 2 minutes. Remove from oven. Let cool. Cut pizza into strips with pizza cutter.

chickaDEE tip: Throw a Lickety-Split Pizza party with your friends! Put out different pizza crust shapes and bowls of toppings.

Make a

Meal

Mmmmmac
& Cheese Dinner

It's easier to make the cold foods first, so here's the plan:

1. Make Tropical Fruit Kebabs.

2. Cook the pasta.

3. Make the salad while the Mmmmmac & Cheese bakes.

MMMM!

Tropical Fruit Kebabs

Prep: 20 minutes

You'll need:

2 bananas

2 mangoes

1 fresh pineapple or 1 can pineapple chunks

6 skewers

sweetened, shredded coconut

1. Peel and cut fruit into **bite-sized** chunks. Carefully thread alternating kinds of fruit onto different skewers.

2. Pour coconut into wide, shallow bowl. Roll each kebab in coconut. When finished, put kebabs in fridge until ready to eat.

Mmmmmac & Cheese Dinner continued . . . ▶

M m m m mac & Cheese

Prep: 60 minutes

You'll need:

750 mL (3 cups) dry, uncooked small pasta (try using shells, bowties or any other favourite shape)

30 mL (2 tbsp) butter

1 clove garlic, chopped

30 mL (2 tbsp) all-purpose flour

500 mL (2 cups) milk

salt and pepper to taste

500 mL (2 cups) grated cheddar cheese

For topping:

125 mL (½ cup) grated cheddar cheese

75 mL (⅓ cup) bread crumbs

1. **Preheat** oven to 180°C (350°F). Grease a 9"x13" casserole dish.

2. Fill large pasta pot with water. Bring to a **boil**. Add pasta and cook for 8 to 10 minutes, stirring from time to time.

Bubble bubble

3. When pasta is ready, ask a helper to **drain** pasta, but *do not rinse*. Put pasta back in pot and cover.

drip! drip!

4. Meanwhile, in medium-sized pan, **melt** butter over medium-low heat. Add garlic and cook for 2 to 3 minutes. **Whisk** in flour to make a paste.

← HOT!

5. Keep stirring and add milk slowly. The paste will get thin. Add salt and pepper. Bring to a **boil** over medium-low heat, and **stir** every minute or so.

6. When the mixture boils, pour it over cooked pasta. Add grated cheese and stir well. Pour pasta into casserole dish.

sploosh

7. **Stir** remaining cheese and bread crumbs together. Sprinkle evenly over pasta. **Bake** for 30 minutes or until golden.

Shelldon's Salad

1. Wash and dry vegetables.

Prep: 15 minutes
You'll need:
1 head of leaf or romaine lettuce
2 tomatoes
1 English cucumber
1 yellow pepper
3 to 4 radishes
1 stalk crisp celery

2. Tear lettuce into bite-sized pieces and place in large salad bowl. Cut other vegetables into bite-sized pieces and add to bowl.

3. Make Drippy Dressing and add to salad just before serving.

Drippy Dressing

1. **Stir** oil, vinegar and mustard together with fork.

Prep: 10 minutes
You'll need:
50 mL (¼ cup) olive oil
15 mL (1 tbsp) wine vinegar
2 mL (½ tsp) Dijon or other sharp mustard
salt and pepper

2. Add *5 shakes* of salt and *2 shakes* of pepper and stir again.

3. Add a little dressing at a time to salad and **toss**. Store leftover dressing in refrigerator.

Sloppy Supper

MENU

Sloppy Brunos

Veggies and Dip

Baked Apples
with vanilla ice cream

Makes: dinner for 6

Here's the plan:

1. Make Baked Apples.

2. While they're baking, cut up the vegetables and make the Sloppy Brunos.

3. Ask someone else to set the table, because after all, you're the chef!

Sloppy Supper continued . . . ▶

Baked Apples

Prep: 10 minutes	
Baking time: 45 minutes	
You'll need:	
6 large washed apples, spy or golden delicious are best	
80 mL (⅓ cup) packed brown sugar	
5 mL (1 tsp) cinnamon	
30 mL (2 tbsp) butter	
vanilla ice cream	

1. **Preheat** oven to 180°C (350°F).

2. Use apple corer to remove core of each apple. Leave about 3 cm (1 in) of apple core at the bottom so filling doesn't run out. Save the tops.

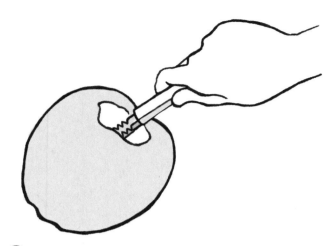

3. Line baking pan with parchment paper or **grease** with butter. Place apples in pan.

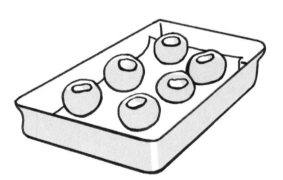

4. **Stir** sugar and cinnamon together. Divide sugar mixture between the 6 apples, and fill each hole.

5. Add 5 mL (1 tsp) of butter to each hole. Cover with apple top.

6. **Bake** for 45 minutes. **Serve** warm with vanilla ice cream!

Veggies and Dip

Prep: 10 minutes

You'll need:

Colourful vegetables such as: cucumbers, baby carrots, broccoli and cauliflower florets, yellow peppers, celery

Your favourite dip

1. Cut vegetables.

2. Arrange vegetables on serving dish with your favourite dips. Ranch and spinach dip are yummy. Try hummus or eggplant dip to shake things up!

chippity chop

Sloppy Brunos

Prep: 30 minutes

You'll need:

15 mL (1 tbsp) vegetable oil

1 onion, chopped

1 clove garlic, chopped

1 rib celery, chopped

1 small red pepper, chopped

2 mL (½ tsp) oregano

salt and pepper to taste

454 g (1 lb) ground turkey

375 mL (1½ cups) crushed tomatoes, canned

5 mL (1 tsp) chili powder

6 kaiser buns

1. **Heat** oil in large pan over medium heat. Add onion and garlic and cook for 3 minutes or until onion softens. Add celery and red pepper and cook for another 3 minutes. Stir in oregano, salt and pepper.

2. Add ground turkey and **stir** for 7 to 10 minutes or until meat is browned.

3. **Stir** in crushed tomatoes and chili powder. **Simmer** for 5 to 10 minutes, until thickened.

4. Toast buns. Scoop a big spoonful of filling onto the bottom of each bun. Top with the other half of the bun. **Serve** with plenty of napkins!

Winter Warmer
Sweet and Spicy Dinner

MENU

Meaty Mini-Pies

Hurry Curry Pumpkin Soup

Chocolate pudding: Serve store-bought pudding – you've worked hard enough!

Makes: dinner for 6

Here's the plan:

1. Make the Meaty Mini-Pies.

2. While they're baking, whisk together the soup.

3. Serve with a smile.

If you don't have time to make the Meaty Mini-Pies in one day, make the filling one day and then fill the pies and bake them the next.

Meaty Mini-Pies

Makes: about 12 small meat pies (you could also make 1 large pie and slice it)

Prep: 30 minutes

Baking time: 25 to 35 minutes

You'll need:

2 packages frozen tart shells (or 2 frozen large pie shells)

50 mL (¼ cup) raisins

30 mL (2 tbsp) chopped dried apricots

15 mL (1 tbsp) vegetable oil

½ cooking onion, chopped

2 mL (½ tsp) ground cinnamon

0.5 mL (⅛ tsp) ground cloves

227 g (½ lb) lean ground beef

2 mL (½ tsp) salt

1 mL (¼ tsp) pepper

1 egg

1. Remove pie shells from freezer and thaw.

2. Mix raisins and apricots in small bowl and cover with warm water. Set aside until ready to use.

3. In large pan, **heat** oil over medium-low heat. Add onion and cook 5 minutes or until soft. **Stir** in cinnamon and cloves.

4. Add beef and turn up heat to medium. Break up meat with the back of a spoon. Add salt and pepper and stir. **Cook** for 5 to 10 minutes or until browned.

5. Drain dried fruit. Add fruit to meat mixture and stir. Turn off heat and let **cool**.

drip drip

SO FAR, SO GOOD!

Meaty Mini-Pies continued . . . ▶

YEAH!

6. Spoon 50 mL (1/4 cup) of filling into each tart shell. **Beat** egg in a small bowl. Use pastry brush to brush a little egg around the edge of each filled pie.

7. To make the tops, remove remaining tart shells from foil cups. Flip upside down on top of each pie and press down gently with your palm. Use your thumb to press the edges together.

8. Gently poke the tops with a fork to make tiny holes for steam to escape. Brush tops with beaten egg.

9. Place cookie sheet in fridge to chill. **Preheat** oven to 190°C (375°F).

10. **Bake** for 20 to 25 minutes or until golden brown. Let cool. Bake a large pie for 45 to 50 minutes.

MAYBE **TOO** GOOD! LET'S EAT THESE OURSELVES!

YEAH!

Hurry Curry Pumpkin Soup

1. **Whisk** together all ingredients except cream or milk in large saucepan. Bring to a boil, then turn heat to low. Let soup cook for about 5 minutes.

Prep: 15 minutes

You'll need:

250 mL (1 cup) canned pumpkin purée
625 mL (2½ cups) beef broth
15 mL (1 tbsp) honey
1 mL (¼ tsp) black pepper
5 mL (1 tsp) salt (no salt if using canned broth)
1 mL (¼ tsp) curry powder
250 mL (1 cup) light cream or milk
croutons, optional

2. Turn heat off and **whisk** in cream or milk. Ladle soup into bowls.

3. Float some croutons on top of each bowl before serving if you wish.

Bon appetit!

Party

Time!

Tobogganing Picnic

Hambake and Jambake

Makes: 8 filled rolls	
Prep: 20 minutes	
You'll need:	
1 package ready-to-bake crescent roll dough	
4 thin slices of ham	
4 thin slices of cheese (cheddar, havarti or Swiss)	
peanut butter	
jam	

1. Preheat oven to 190°C (375°F). Line cookie sheet with parchment paper. Unroll dough and separate triangles.

2. Spread thin layer of peanut butter and jam on 4 triangles. Roll up according to package directions.

3. For remaining triangles, roll each slice of cheese in a slice of ham, then place in centre of each triangle. Roll up according to package directions.

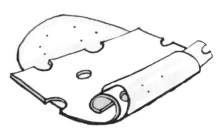

4. **Bake** for 10 to 12 minutes, or until golden. **Cool** on rack. Eat warm, or wrap in tin foil to take with you.

Tobogganing Picnic continued . . . ▶

Creamy Mashed Potato Soup

Makes: 8 cups
Prep: 1 hour
You'll need:
2 leeks
1 kg (2 lb) (4 large) peeled potatoes
30 mL (2 tbsp) butter
1.5 L (6 cups) water
5 mL (1 tsp) salt
1 mL (¼ tsp) pepper
175 mL (¾ cup) 10% cream

1. **Trim** leeks so you're left with white and soft, green parts. Cut in half lengthwise and wash well, rinsing dirt between leaves. **Chop.** Cut potatoes into small chunks.

2. In large pot, **melt** butter over medium-low heat. Add leeks and stir until coated with butter. **Cook** for 5 minutes or until soft, stirring now and then.

3. Add potatoes and stir. Add water, salt and pepper. Bring to a **boil** and then turn to low. Cover and **cook** for about 35 minutes.

4. **Pour** soup into a blender or food processor and **purée** until smooth. Carefully pour it back into the pot. **Stir** in cream. Warm over low heat, but don't **boil.**

WRRRR

5. **Pour** into thermos and get ready to hit the hills! You'll have leftovers.

Hot Chocolate

1. **Whisk** cocoa mix into hot milk in a large pot.

2. **Pour** into a thermos. Take marshmallows to add later!

Makes: 6 cups
Prep: 5 minutes
You'll need:
160 mL (⅔ cup) cocoa mix from page 83
1.25 L (5 cups) milk
marshmallows

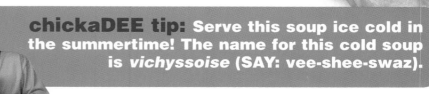

chickaDEE tip: Serve this soup ice cold in the summertime! The name for this cold soup is *vichyssoise* (SAY: vee-shee-swaz).

Brown Sugar Shortbread

Makes: about 30 cookies

Prep: 45 minutes

You'll need:

500 mL (2 cups) all-purpose flour
1 mL (¼ tsp) salt
250 mL (1 cup) unsalted butter, softened
125 mL (½ cup) packed brown sugar
5 mL (1 tsp) vanilla

1. **Preheat** oven to 160°C (325°F). Line a cookie sheet with parchment paper.

2. **Stir** flour and salt together in small bowl. Set aside.

3. In large bowl, cream butter with electric mixer until light and fluffy.

4. Add sugar and beat for 3 minutes. **Scrape** sides of bowl with spatula. **Beat** in vanilla.

Bzzz

5. Add flour and salt to butter mixture and beat on low until combined. Dough should stick together when squeezed.

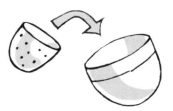

6. Shape dough into small balls and place on cookie sheet, about 4 cm (1½ in) apart. Flatten slightly with a fork.

smooooosh

7. **Bake** 15 to 20 minutes until firm. **Cool** for 10 minutes on cookie sheet. Remove from sheet and continue to cool.

Dee's Sleepover Extravaganza

MENU
Peach Fizz
Totally Terrific Taco Buffet with Get Up & Guacamole
Banana Split Bar
Breakfast Pizza
Serves: 6 sleepers

PEEK!

Z Z Z Z Z z z z

Peach Fizz

Makes: 6 drinks

Prep: 10 minutes

You'll need:

250 mL (1 cup) coarse red sugar

Sparkling peach or peach-apple juice

Berry juice or fruit punch

6 fancy glasses

1. Pour sugar into small bowl. Put 2 cm (1½ in) of water in another bowl.

2. Dip rim of a glass into the water. Dip wet rim into sugar until it is coated. Put glass on table, right side up and let dry. Repeat for all 6 glasses.

3. Carefully fill each glass about half full with sparkling peach juice. Add berry juice for colour.

Get Up & Guacamole

1. Cut avocados in half and remove pits. Scoop avocado into bowl and mash.

Makes: about 2 cups

Prep: 10 minutes

You'll need:

2 ripe avocados

1 lime

5 mL (1 tsp) salt

pepper to taste

Optional:

1 clove of garlic, crushed

1 ripe tomato, finely chopped

125 mL (½ cup) cilantro leaves, chopped

2. Cut lime in half and squeeze juice into small bowl. **Pour** juice over avocados and blend with salt and pepper.

3. Add any optional ingredients you want.

PSST! WAKE UP, GUYS! LET'S EAT SOMETHING!

Sleepover continued . . .

chickaDEE tip: Make a Tex-Mex party! Buy a candy-filled piñata, wear sombreros and play Mexican musical chairs!

Totally Terrific Taco Buffet

Makes: 12 tacos

Prep: 45 minutes

You'll need:

12 taco shells

30 mL (2 tbsp) vegetable oil

454 g (1 lb) lean ground beef

1 yellow onion, chopped

5 mL (1 tsp) oregano

5 mL (1 tsp) salt

1 mL (¼ tsp) cumin

1 mL (¼ tsp) pepper

Fillings:

sour cream

½ head lettuce, shredded

500 mL (2 cups) cheddar cheese, grated (or buy pre-grated cheese)

store-bought salsa

Get Up & Guacamole (see recipe on page 53)

1. Place fillings in serving bowls on table.

2. For meat filling, **heat** oil in large saucepan over medium-low. Add onion, and stir. Cover pan. **Stir** occasionally with wooden spoon until onions are soft and clear.

3. Measure spices in small bowl, then add to onions. Add beef and break up with the back of a spoon.

4. Cook for 10 minutes, until meat is brown with no pink spots. Spoon meat into a large bowl and place on table.

5. Warm taco shells in oven at 150°C (300°F) for about 3 minutes. Now invite all your guests to make their own Totally Terrific Tacos.

Banana Split Bar

Makes: A lot!

You'll need:

banana split dishes or ice-cream bowls

spoons

lots of napkins

3 flavours of ice cream: try butterscotch, cherry and chocolate chip

peeled bananas, sliced in half lengthwise

sweet sauces: chocolate, butterscotch, marshmallow whip, whipped cream

colourful candies for toppings: gummy snakes, chocolate chips, jelly beans, ju-jubes, coloured sugar sprinkles, candy bar pieces

Breakfast Pizza

Makes: 6 pizzas

You'll need:

6 small whole wheat pita breads

cream cheese

peanut butter

thinly sliced fruit: bananas, apples, kiwis, mandarin oranges, strawberries

other toppings: cereal, granola, raisins, almonds, dried fruits like papaya, apricots, raisins or dates . . . or whatever else you want

1. Spread cream cheese or peanut butter on pita.

2. Cover with sliced fruit and other toppings.

3. Slice breakfast pizzas into triangles. **Serve** with orange juice and a helping of Saturday morning cartoons!

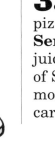

Summer Sprinkler Party

MENU

Real Lemonade

S'more Sandwiches

Fruit Freeze Ups

Petal Pops

Serves: 8 really hot kids

WHEE!

REFRESHING!

Real Lemonade

1. Squeeze lemons to make 375 mL (1½ cups) of juice. Set aside.

Makes: 750 mL (3 cups) of lemon syrup, or 8 glasses of lemonade	
Prep: 20 minutes, plus a few hours to chill	
You'll need:	
6 lemons	
250 mL (1 cup) water	
375 mL (1½ cups) sugar	
1.25 L (5 cups) cold water	
extra thin slices of lemon to garnish	

2. **Stir** 250 mL (1 cup) water and sugar in small saucepan. Bring to a **boil** over medium-high heat. Remove from heat and stir until sugar is dissolved. Let **cool**.

3. **Stir** sugar syrup into lemon juice and refrigerate until chilled.

4. **Pour** lemon syrup in a pitcher and add 1.25 L (5 cups) of cold water.

yum!

chickaDEE tip: For fizzy lemonade use soda water instead of plain water. Decorate glasses with lemon slices.

Sprinkler Party continued . . . ▶

S'more Sandwiches

GIMME S'MORE!

ARF! ARF!

Makes: 8 sandwiches

Prep: 20 minutes, plus 1 hour in the freezer

You'll need:

chocolate ice cream in a box

16 graham crackers

250 mL (1 cup) marshmallow whip

chocolate sprinkles

1. Open ice cream box. Use a sharp knife to cut the ice cream into slices 2.5 cm (1 in) thick and the same width as the crackers. Cut 1 square for each sandwich.

2. On 1 side of 1 graham cracker, spread some marshmallow whip. Place an ice-cream slice on top of the marshmallow layer. Top with another graham cracker.

3. Pour chocolate sprinkles into a shallow plate. Press all 4 edges of the sandwich into the sprinkles.

4. Wrap each sandwich in plastic wrap and place in the freezer for an hour.

Fruit Freeze Ups

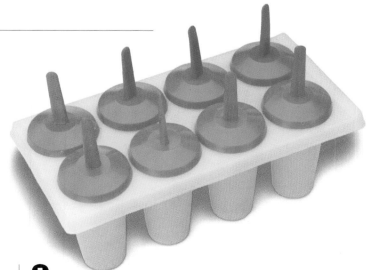

Makes: 8 pops

Prep: 10 minutes, plus overnight in the freezer

You'll need:

250 mL (1 cup) fruit punch

10 to 12 strawberries, washed and hulled

½ banana

1. Put all ingredients into the blender or food processor and blend until smooth.

2. Pour mixture into eight ice pop molds. **Freeze** overnight.

Petal Pops

Makes: 9 banana pops

Prep: 20 minutes, plus at least 2 hours in the freezer

You'll need:

3 bananas

9 sticks

500 mL (2 cups) semi-sweet chocolate chips

250 mL (1 cup) sprinkles, chopped nuts, candy sequins or other edible decorations

MHO MOOK A MITE *MOUT* MOF MA MAMANNA? MIE MON'T MOW.

1. Line a large cookie sheet with waxed paper. Peel bananas and cut each into 3 pieces. Push a stick partway into each chunk and put on cookie sheet. Place in freezer until frozen.

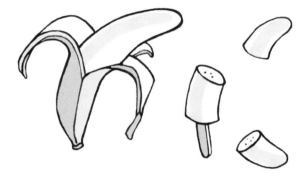

2. Heat 4 cm (2 in) of water in a saucepan. Remove from heat. Place a metal mixing bowl onto rim of saucepan. The bottom of the bowl should be over the water, but not sitting in it. **Pour** chocolate chips into bowl. **Stir** until melted.

3. Pour decorations onto a shallow plate. Dip each frozen banana into melted chocolate. Use the back of a spoon to help coat each banana.

4. Roll each chocolatey banana in decorations. Place back on waxed paper. Put cookie sheet in freezer for 2 hours or overnight.

DEE Desserts

licious
& Breads

Swirly Twirly
Cinnamunch

VERY STICKY, VERY *YUMMY!*

Makes: one large loaf

Prep: 2¾ hours total
work time: 45 minutes
rising time: 1½ hours
baking time: 30 minutes

You'll need:

For the dough:

50 mL (¼ cup) warm water

50 mL (¼ cup plus a pinch) white sugar

1 package dry active yeast

30 mL (2 tbsp) unsalted butter

5 mL (1 tsp) salt

175 mL (¾ cup) warm milk

2 large eggs

875 mL (3½ cups) all-purpose flour

For the coating:

175 mL (¾ cup) packed brown sugar

125 mL (½ cup) chopped walnuts or pecans

10 mL (2 tsp) cinnamon

125 mL (½ cup) unsalted butter

For the icing:

30 mL (2 tbsp) milk

300 mL (1¼ cup) icing sugar

1. *Make the dough:* **Pour** warm water in small bowl and add pinch of sugar. Sprinkle yeast on top and **stir** gently. Set aside for 10 minutes or until yeast is dissolved and looks foamy. Butter a 10-inch Bundt pan and a medium bowl.

2. Put remaining white sugar, butter, salt, warm milk and eggs in a mixing bowl. **Pour** in yeast mixture and **mix** well with dough hooks of an electric mixer or by hand with a wooden spoon.

3. Add flour slowly and mix on low speed. Once dough is blended, **knead** with electric mixer for 1 minute or with your hands for 5 minutes.

brrrrr

4. Pat sticky dough into a ball and place in buttered bowl. Turn it over once, and then cover with a clean cloth. Set aside for 20 minutes.

5. *Make the coating:* **Mix** brown sugar, nuts and cinnamon in a small bowl. **Melt** butter and place in another bowl.

cinn

brown sugar

BUTTER

6. After 20 minutes, take dough out of bowl and cut into 4 equal pieces. Roll each piece into a log, and cut each log into 12 pieces. Roll each piece into a ball.

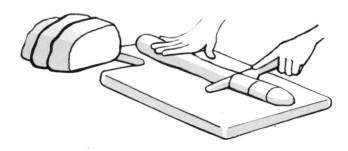

7. Make an assembly line. With one hand, dip a ball into the butter. Then with the other hand, roll it around in the sugar mixture. Stack the balls of dough close together in the buttered Bundt pan.

8. Cover the pan with a clean cloth, and set in warm place to rise for 1 to 1½ hours. It should double in size.

9. **Preheat** oven to 180°C (350°F). **Bake** for 30 minutes or until golden brown. When done, remove from oven. Let cool in pan for about 20 minutes. Then, turn upside down on a serving plate. Allow to **cool** completely before icing.

10. *Make the icing:* Stir icing sugar and milk together in small bowl until smooth. Use a spoon to drizzle icing over bread. Let it dribble into centre and outside of bread.

Raisin Rounds

Makes: about 24 biscuits

Prep: 1 hour

You'll need:

750 mL (3 cups) all-purpose flour
15 mL (1 tbsp) baking powder
2 mL (½ tsp) baking soda
2 mL (½ tsp) salt
7 mL (1½ tsp) sugar
175 mL (¾ cup) cold, unsalted butter
375 mL (1½ cups) buttermilk
125 mL (½ cup) packed raisins

1. **Preheat** oven to 190°C (375°F). Line 2 cookie sheets with parchment paper.

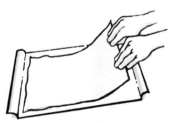

2. **Measure** flour, baking powder, baking soda, salt and sugar into food processor. **Blend** on low for a minute until combined.

3. Cut butter into small pieces. Add to food processor and blend on medium-low speed for 5 seconds at a time. Stop when mixture looks like fat bread crumbs.

4. **Pour** mixture into large mixing bowl and stir in buttermilk. The dough will be sticky. Stir in raisins.

HA HA HA!

HUFF!

5. Put dough on a floured cutting board and sprinkle with a little flour. Use your hands to pat dough until it is 1 1/2 cm (1/2 in) thick.

6. Use a drinking glass or 6 cm (2 1/2 in) round cookie cutter to cut out dough rounds. Place rounds on cookie sheet. Gather dough scraps, pat them again and cut more rounds.

7. **Bake** rounds for 15 minutes, until slightly golden. Cool on cookie sheets for 5 minutes. Transfer to cooling rack.

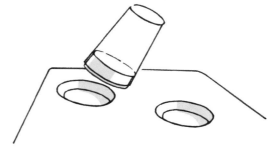

chickaDEE tip: Make birthday biscuits for someone special! Replace the raisins with grated cheese or dried cherries and chocolate chips.

Kooky Cookies

OH, YEAH!

Rocko Chocos

Makes: 12 to 15 large treats, or 20 to 25 little treats

Prep: 25 minutes, plus time to chill

You'll need:

375 mL (1½ cups) semi-sweet chocolate chips

250 mL (1 cup) mini marshmallows

250 mL (1 cup) slivered almonds

80 mL (⅓ cup) white chocolate chips

250 mL (1 cup) crisp rice cereal

1. To **melt** semi-sweet chocolate chips, put in bowl and set over another bowl of hot water. **Stir** until smooth. **Cool** for 10 minutes.

2. **Stir** in remaining **ingredients**.

Tick tock Tick tock...

3. Line cookie sheet with parchment paper. **Drop** rounded tablespoons of chocolate mixture onto cookie sheet, about 5 cm (2 in) apart.

4. **Place** cookie sheet in refrigerator until set. Cookies can be stored in covered container for about a week, if they last that long!

Spiders

Makes: 4 cookies

Prep: 10 minutes

You'll need:

4 cream sandwich cookies

12 pieces of licorice or string licorice, cut in half

pre-made icing or nut butter

coloured candies

1. Open cookie and place 8 licorice halves for legs on cookie bottom.

2. Replace cookie top. Glue 2 candies for eyes using icing or nut butter. Repeat for each cookie.

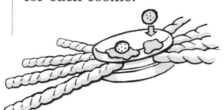

U.F.O. Crunch

Makes: 4 cookies

Prep: 15 minutes

You'll need:

4 large cookies

pre-made icing

2 doughnut balls, cut in half

coloured candies

4 pieces of licorice, cut in half

1. Cover cookie with icing.

2. Place half a doughnut ball in the middle of each cookie.

3. Stick 2 half pieces of licorice in doughnut. Place candies around rim.

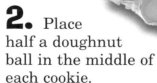

4. Repeat for each U.F.O.

Yogurt Arf-ait

Makes: 4 servings

Prep: 10 minutes

You'll need:

4 seedless mandarin oranges, sliced *or* 2 cans mandarin oranges, drained

125 mL (½ cup) chopped almonds

250 mL (1 cup) vanilla yogurt

chocolate syrup

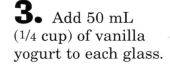

3. Add 50 mL (1/4 cup) of vanilla yogurt to each glass.

2. Add 15 mL (1 tbsp) of almonds to each glass.

1. Divide mandarins in half. Put first half equally in bottoms of 4 glasses.

4. Add another layer of mandarin slices. Top with chocolate syrup and 15 mL (1 tbsp) of almonds. Refrigerate until ready to serve.

chickaDEE tip:
Try Blueberry Arf-aits**! In this order, layer the bottom of a glass with Yummy Blueberry Sauce (page 13), granola and vanilla yogurt. Top with more Blueberry Sauce and granola. Or, how about** Banana Maple Walnut Arf-aits**? Layer sliced bananas, chopped walnuts and vanilla yogurt. Drizzle with maple syrup.**

Perfectly Peachy Crisp

Makes: 6 servings

Prep: 15 minutes

Baking time: 35 to 40 minutes

You'll need:

Peach mixture:

2 cans sliced peaches in juice, each 796 mL (27 oz)

80 mL (2 tbsp) flour

75 mL (⅓ cup) brown sugar

Topping:

125 mL (½ cup) all-purpose flour

175 mL (¾ cup) large-flake rolled oats

2 mL (½ tsp) salt

125 mL (½ cup) brown sugar

125 mL (½ cup) unsalted butter

chickaDEE tip: You could replace the peaches with other fruit, like apples or berries.

1. **Preheat** oven to 180°C (350°F). **Grease** 2 L (8 cup) casserole dish.

2. *For peach mixture:* **Drain** peaches in sieve. In large mixing bowl, stir peaches, flour and brown sugar together. Set aside.

3. *For topping:* **Mix** flour, oats and salt in another bowl. Crumble in brown sugar with your fingers to get rid of lumps. **Melt** butter in saucepan. **Pour** over flour mixture. **Stir**.

4. Spoon peaches into casserole. Use your hands to crumble topping mixture over fruit. Bake 35 to 40 minutes, until golden and bubbling. **Cool** on rack. **Serve** warm with vanilla ice cream or frozen yogurt.

Cups o' Cake

Makes: 12 cupcakes

Prep: 1 hour

You'll need:

175 mL (3/4 cup) unsweetened cocoa
250 mL (1 cup) all-purpose flour
5 mL (1 tsp) baking powder
1 mL (1/4 tsp) salt
175 mL (3/4 cup) unsalted butter, at room temperature
250 mL (1 cup) sugar
2 large eggs
5 mL (1 tsp) vanilla
125 mL (1/2 cup) milk

1. **Preheat** oven to 180°C (350°F). Line 12 muffin cups with paper liners.

2. Sift cocoa, flour, baking powder and salt together. Set aside.

3. In large bowl, cream butter and sugar with electric mixer until light and fluffy. Add eggs one at a time, beating well. **Beat** in vanilla.

Cool Icing

Mix the icing up while your Cups o' Cake are baking!

Prep: 15 minutes

You'll need:

250 mL (1 cup) unsalted butter, at room temperature

750 mL (3 cups) icing sugar

50 mL (¼ cup) light cream

food colouring

candy decorations

1. Cream butter with an electric mixer. Add icing sugar slowly until mixture is fluffy. Add cream and beat well.

2. Separate icing into smaller bowls and **beat** different food colouring into each. Keep adding until it's the colour you want.

5. Spoon batter into muffin cups. **Bake** for 25 minutes, or until a toothpick inserted into the centre of a cupcake comes out clean. **Cool** on rack.

4. Add half the flour mixture and **beat.** Add milk and beat. Add the remaining flour mixture and beat for 3 minutes.

3. Spread icing on cupcakes when they are completely cool. Add candy decorations.

Kitchen

Gifts

THAT'S RIGHT!

A GINGERBREAD NECK-LACE AND A STAINED GLASS COOKIE! COOL!

NO. THESE ARE FOR US! WE GOT BRUNO THE CHICKADEE COOKBOOK!

MUNCH!

MUNCH!

Eat it Up!

END

Soup in a Jar

Makes: 1 jar of pasta and pea soup

Prep: 10 minutes

You'll need:

125 mL (½ cup) yellow split peas

125 mL (½ cup) small pasta

125 mL (½ cup) red lentils

125 mL (½ cup) pearl barley

30 mL (2 tbsp) dried parsley

30 mL (2 tbsp) dried onion

5 mL (1 tsp) dried thyme

5 mL (1 tsp) dried oregano

Special equipment:

glass pint jar

ribbon

cooking instruction label

1. **Pour** half the split peas in jar. Then layer half the pasta, half the lentils and half the barley. Sprinkle dried parsley around edges. Repeat layering with remaining peas, pasta, lentils and barley. Sprinkle dried onion around edges. Top with thyme and oregano.

2. Close lid tightly and tie with ribbon. Make an instruction label and tie to jar. You can create your own original label or photocopy this one and decorate it.

○ **Soup in a Jar**

To:

From:

Add this soup mix to 2 litres (8 cups) of soup stock or water in a large pot and bring to a boil. Reduce heat to low, cover the pot, and simmer for 50 minutes or until the split peas are tender.

Happy slurping!

Stained-Glass Cookies

THESE COOKIES ARE ALMOST TOO BEAUTIFUL TO EAT!

Makes: 2 to 3 dozen cookies

Prep: 1 hour

You'll need:

1 L (4 cups) hard candies, in a variety of colours
500 mL (2 cups) all-purpose flour
2 mL (½ tsp) salt
2 mL (½ tsp) baking powder
125 mL (½ cup) unsalted butter, soft
250 mL (1 cup) sugar
1 egg
5 mL (1 tsp) vanilla

1. **Preheat** oven to 180°C (350°F). Line several cookie sheets with parchment paper. Crush candies of the same colour separately by placing in sealed sandwich bags and hitting with a mallet. Put each colour in a separate bowl.

crunch crackle

2. **Stir** flour, salt and baking powder together. Set aside. In large bowl, cream butter with sugar until light and fluffy. **Beat** in egg and vanilla. Add flour mixture and **mix** on low speed.

3. Roll dough out to 1/2 cm (1/4 in) thick on a floured surface. Use large cookie cutters to cut shapes then transfer to the cookie sheets.

4. Use small cookie cutters or a sharp knife to cut shapes out of the middles of unbaked cookies. Fill each hole completely with crushed candies. **Bake** for 7 to 9 minutes, until edges are golden brown and candies are melted. Gently lift the cookies off the sheets when completely cool.

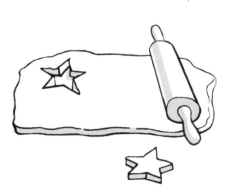

chickaDEE tip: Use a straw to make a hole in the tops of unbaked cookies to make stained-glass pendants!

Gingerbread **Puzzle**

CUTE LITTLE FELLOW!

Makes: 3 puzzles

Prep: 1 hour

You'll need:

750 mL (3 cups) all-purpose flour
2 mL (½ tsp) baking soda
2 mL (½ tsp) salt
125 mL (½ cup) unsalted butter, soft
125 mL (½ cup) packed brown sugar
10 mL (2 tsp) ground ginger
10 mL (2 tsp) cinnamon
2 mL (½ tsp) ground cloves
1 egg
125 mL (½ cup) molasses

1. **Preheat** oven to 180°C (350°F). Line several cookie sheets with parchment paper.

2. In large bowl, **stir** flour, baking soda and salt together.

3. In another large bowl, cream butter and sugar until light and fluffy. **Mix** in the spices, then the egg and molasses.

4. Add flour to butter mixture and **beat** until combined. Pat dough together and divide into 3 balls. Work with 1 at a time.

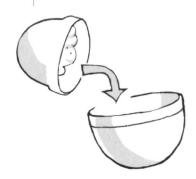

5. Flatten 1 ball of dough. Roll out on floured tabletop. It should be less than 1 cm (1/2 in) thick. Trim into a large square or rectangle shape with a knife.

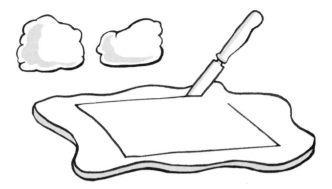

6. Transfer dough onto cookie sheet using a wide spatula. **Bake** about 12 minutes. Remove from oven. Let cool 2 minutes. Use a pizza cutter to cut into shapes but *do not separate*. Let cookie sheet cool on a rack.

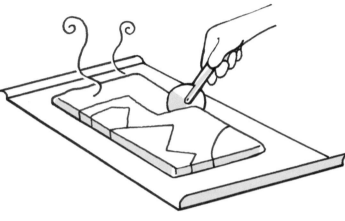

7. When cool, decorate puzzle with icing (see recipe at right). Pull pieces apart to dry. Pack into a box with tissue and tie with ribbon.

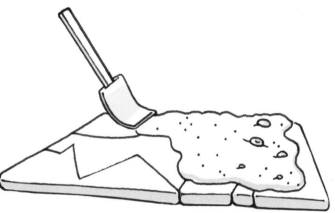

Cookie Icing

Prep: 15 minutes

You'll need:

454 g (1 lb or 3½ cups) icing sugar

75 mL (5 tbsp) meringue powder – check the baking aisle

125 mL (½ cup) water

food colouring (optional)

1. **Beat** ingredients with electric mixer for about 7 minutes, or until fluffy.

2. Use immediately in an icing bag or with a small brush. Store leftovers in an airtight container.

chickaDEE tip: Make gingerbread jewellery! Preheat oven to 180°C (350°F). Roll one ball of the dough on a floured tabletop. Cut shapes using very small cookie cutters. For earrings or pendants, make a hole in the top part of each shape with a straw. Transfer shapes to a cookie sheet and bake for 7 minutes. When cool, tie yarn through holes or get an adult to help you attach safety pins to make brooches.

Hot Cider Sacks

Makes: 6 sacks

Prep: 15 minutes

You'll need:

6 cinnamon sticks

30 whole cardamom pods

30 whole cloves

18 slices of crystallized ginger, about 3 cm (1¼ in) each

Special equipment:

cheesecloth

kitchen twine

glass pint jar

MY TEACHER IS GOING TO LOVE THESE!

1. **Cut** out six 13 cm (5 in) squares of cheesecloth. Lay them out on a large work surface.

snippity snip

2. Break each cinnamon stick into 3 pieces. Place 3 cinnamon stick pieces, 5 cardamom pods, 5 cloves and 3 pieces of ginger on each square of cheesecloth.

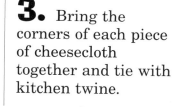

3. Bring the corners of each piece of cheesecloth together and tie with kitchen twine.

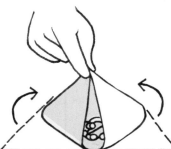

4. Pack the sacks into a jar with these instructions: For mulled cider, simmer 2 L (8 cups) of apple cider with one sack in a covered pot for 30 minutes. Serve in mugs.

Cocoa and Spoons

Makes: 1 cup of cocoa mix and 12 spoons
Prep: 20 minutes
You'll need:
125 mL (½ cup) unsweetened cocoa
125 mL (½ cup) sugar
250 mL (1 cup) semi-sweet chocolate chips
12 sturdy plastic spoons
Special equipment:
250 mL (1 cup) glass jar
ribbon

The Mix

1. **Sift** cocoa and sugar together.

2. **Pour** into jar and seal. Attach label which reads: Mix 22 mL (1½ tbsp) of cocoa mix with 250 mL (1 cup) hot milk for a steamy treat!

SLURP!

The Spoons

1. **Melt** chocolate chips in a bowl over hot, but not boiling, water. Dip each spoon into melted chocolate. Be sure that the bowl of each spoon is completely coated.

2. Stand each spoon in a drinking glass (chocolate side up!) and refrigerate for 30 minutes until hardened. Tie spoons to jar with ribbon. Give as a gift with the cocoa mix.

Chewy Gooey Candy Apples

Makes: 8 candy apples

Prep: 45 minutes

You'll need:

8 small apples

250 mL (1 cup) sugar

50 mL (¼ cup) dark corn syrup

250 mL (1 cup) whipping cream

30 mL (2 tbsp) butter

Special equipment:

sticks

candy thermometer

cellophane

ribbon

HERE'S ANOTHER ONE!